Lee Aucoin, *Creative Director*
Jamey Acosta, *Senior Editor*
Heidi Fiedler, *Editor*
Produced and designed by
Denise Ryan & Associates
Illustration © Mike Brownlow
Rachelle Cracchiolo, *Publisher*

Teacher Created Materials

5301 Oceanus Drive
Huntington Beach, CA 92649-1030
http://www.tcmpub.com
Paperback: ISBN: 978-1-4333-5527-1
Library Binding: ISBN: 978-1-4807-1695-7
© 2014 Teacher Created Materials
Printed in China
Nordica.082019.CA21901407

Journey to the Center of the Earth

Written by Sally Odgers
Illustrated by Mike Brownlow

A strange teacher was waiting when Todd got to school. The teacher had on a strange silver suit. "I'm Mr. Verne," he greeted the children. "We're going to the center."

3

Todd sighed. The Interactive Learning Center was fun but not exciting. "We'll have to write about it," he whispered to his friend Cai.

"Outside, everyone," said Mr. Verne.
"Into my rocket. Put on your safety suits."

"Wow! This is amazing!" said Cai.

"Why do we need safety suits?" asked Todd.
This might be exciting.

"You'll see," said Mr. Verne. "Don't forget
your helmets."

When the children were ready, the rocket took off. Cai grabbed Todd's arm as the rocket shot out over the ocean toward Iceland and a thick plume of smoke.

Todd stared at the smoke. Something glowed underneath. "That's a volcano!" he exclaimed. "It looks as if the ice is on fire!"

"Very good," said Mr. Verne. "That's where we're going."

"You said you were taking us to the center!" gasped Cai.

"I am," said Mr. Verne. "We're going to the center of the Earth!" The rocket dove through choking clouds of smoke. Todd shut his eyes as orange fire spewed around them.

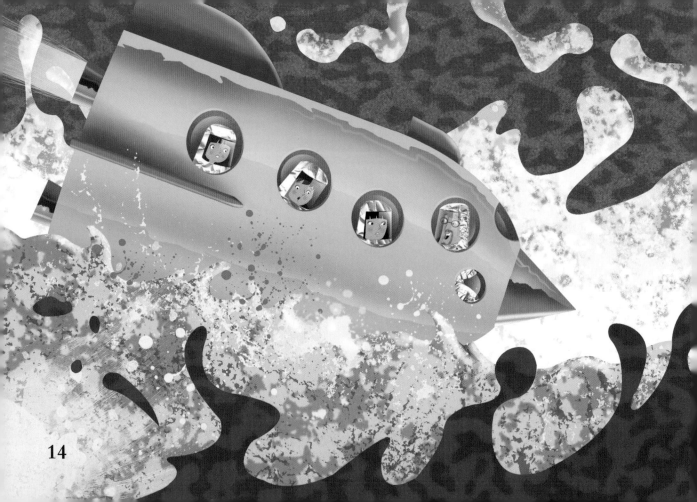

"This is lava. Melted rock," said the professor. "Don't worry. You're safe in the rocket." Todd opened his eyes.

"Now, we're going into the magma," said their teacher. "Magma is the same as lava, except it's under the Earth's crust and hotter—much hotter."

Outside the windows, Todd saw bubbling red rock.

"Because magma is like liquid, the rocket can pass through it," said Mr. Verne. "We can't go through solid rock, so we travel through magma streams." He smiled. "Take notes, everyone."

"I forgot my pencil," said Todd.

The rocket swooped through liquid rock and skidded through slippery tunnels Mr. Verne called lava tubes.

"We're at the center of the Earth," said Mr. Verne. "This is called the Earth's core."

"Like an apple core?" asked Cai.

Mr. Verne laughed. "Not quite. Hold on. We're going up!"

Todd grabbed his seat as the rocket shot through more magma. The glowing orange faded to red. The rocket rose through thick smoke.

"Where are we?" asked Cai as the air cleared.

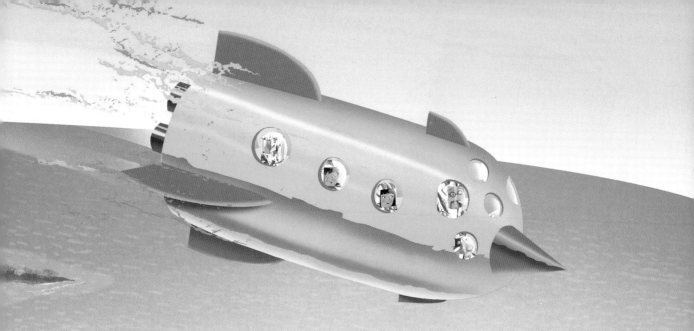

"We've come up through a volcano in Hawaii," said Mr. Verne. "We'll land for lunch. Then, it's back to school."

Todd smiled. He couldn't wait to write about this!